Ten Oni Drummers

by Matthew Gollub

illustrated by Kazuko G. Stone

Lee & Low Books Inc. ✦ New York

In dreams I gaze upon the sand,
beneath the moonlight in Japan.
I taste the salty wind and sea . . .

. . . and sometimes I have company.

One oni by the shore,
rears its head and calls for more.

Two tiny oni creep,
grunt and shake off years of sleep.

Three oni, eyes aglow,
drumming makes them grow and grow.

Ichi, ni, san, TUN-TUN!
One two three, around they run.

Four oni raise their flags,
trample forth from rocky crags.

Five oni sail on swells,
land their rafts and sound their shells.

Six oni stoke their flames,
play their nasty goblin games.

Ichi, *ni*, *san*, TUN-TUN!
One two three, around they run.
Shi, *go*, *roku*, HOH!
Four five six, their red eyes glow.

Seven oni — toothsome grins,
dinner dripping down their chins.

Eight oni pat their tums,
pound their even larger drums.

They drum beneath the blackened skies,
drum to reach enormous size—
pound their giant drums of wood,
drum because it feels so good.

Nine giant oni reach,
climb sheer cliffs above the beach.

Ten oni fierce and tall,
bang their biggest drums of all.

Ichi, ni, san, TUN-TUN!
One two three, around they run.
Shi, go, roku, HOH!
Four five six, their red eyes glow.
Shichi, hachi, ku, ju.
Seven-eight-nine-ten you know who!

To me they're friendly, and what's more,
they stand guard over slumber's shore.

When spooky dreams fill me with fright,
they chase those dreams . . .

Then as daybreak lights the land,
they shrink and sink back in the sand.

Oni (oh-nee) are creatures of great size and strength that have appeared in Japanese folklore for many centuries. The term is often translated as "ogre" or "demon" because oni are usually depicted as fearsome beings with fangs, horns, and loincloths of tiger fur. But oni may also serve as protectors, using their strength and startling appearance to ward off fear and evil. In some regional festivals in Japan, people dressed as oni bang on taiko or lead processions, sweeping evil from the path to protect all who follow.

Taiko (tie-koh) are barrel-shaped Japanese drums. They range in size from as small as a basketball to as large as a car. Traditionally, these drums were used to communicate between villages, to purify the air in religious ceremonies, and even to chase away pests from the fields. Today, most people in Japan hear taiko rhythms at festivals, where men and women drum and shout to excite the entire crowd. Taiko groups have also sprung up outside Japan, and famous taiko troupes travel the world dazzling audiences with their awesome energy and precision.

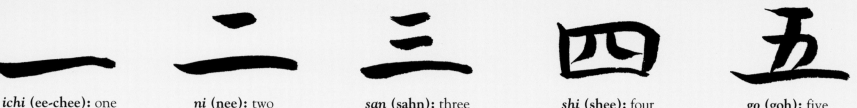

ichi (ee-chee): one · · · · **ni (nee):** two · · · · **san (sahn):** three · · · · **shi (shee):** four · · · · **go (goh):** five

About Kanji

Written Japanese includes thousands of **kanji (kahn-jee),** Chinese characters that the Japanese adopted hundreds of years ago. Almost two billion people around the world can read these characters, and children in many Asian countries begin learning to write kanji in elementary school.

A basic kanji may consist of just one pen stroke. A complicated one may consist of more than twenty strokes. When children learn to write kanji, they must memorize each character's shape as well as the order and direction of the strokes. The chart below shows how to write the kanji for the numbers *one* through *ten*. The arrow shows the direction of each stroke. —M.G.

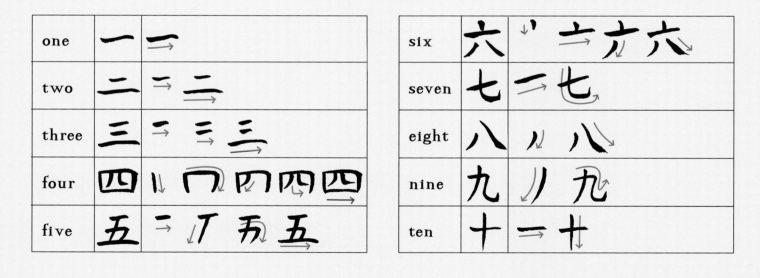

roku (roh-koo): six · · · · **shichi (shee-chee):** seven · · · · **hachi (hah-chee):** eight · · · · **ku (koo** *or* **kyu):** nine · · · · **ju (joo):** ten

To Jacob, who loves taiko, and to my teacher Shoji Ueda of Fukuoka, Japan —M.G.

To Dorian, Kasuga, Fujihiko, Marc and Matthew's family, after whom I modeled my oni

—K.G.S.

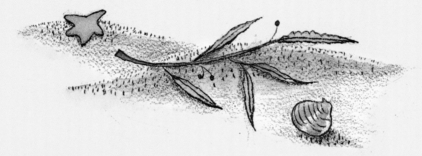

Text copyright © 2000 by Matthew Gollub
Illustrations copyright © 2000 by Kazuko G. Stone

LEE & LOW BOOKS Inc., 95 Madison Avenue, New York, NY 10016
www.leeandlow.com

Printed in the United States of America

Calligraphy by Keiko Smith
Book design by Tania Garcia
Book production by The Kids at Our House

The text is set in Adrift
The illustrations are rendered in watercolor and colored pencil

10 9 8 7 6 5 4 3 2 1

First Edition

Library of Congress Cataloging-in-Publication Data
Gollub, Matthew.
Ten oni drummers / by Matthew Gollub ; illustrations by Kazuko G. Stone.
— 1st ed.   p.   cm.
Summary: One by one, ten tiny oni, Japanese goblin-like creatures,
grow larger and larger as they beat their drums on the sand,
chasing away bad dreams.
ISBN 1-58430-011-6 (hardcover)
[1. Monsters—Fiction. 2. Japan—Fiction. 3. Counting.]
I. Stone, Kazuko G., ill. II. Title.
PZ7.G583 Te 2000
[E]—dc21   00-035416